When The Night Closes In

The Hellion Club
Novella

by Chasity Bowlin

DRAGONBLADE
PUBLISHING, INC.

Dragonblade Publishing, Inc. is an imprint of Kathryn Le Veque Novels, Inc.
P.O. Box 23
Moreno Valley, CA 92556
ceo@dragonbladepublishing.com

Produced in the United States of America

First Edition September 2023
Print Edition

ARE YOU SIGNED UP FOR DRAGONBLADE'S BLOG?

You'll get the latest news and information on exclusive giveaways, exclusive excerpts, coming releases, sales, free books, cover reveals and more.

Check out our complete list of authors, too!

No spam, no junk. That's a promise!

Sign Up Here

www.dragonbladepublishing.com

Dearest Reader;

Thank you for your support of a small press. At Dragonblade Publishing, we strive to bring you the highest quality Historical Romance from some of the best authors in the business. Without your support, there is no 'us', so we sincerely hope you adore these stories and find some new favorite authors along the way.

Happy Reading!

CEO, Dragonblade Publishing

Pirates of Britannia Series
The Pirate's Bluestocking

Also from Chasity Bowlin
Into the Night

Chapter One

NIGHTLEIGH HOUSE WAS more than simply imposing. It was, in a word, terrifying. Ominous. Foreboding. *Evil*. There were, in fact, many words to describe it.

Standing in the circular drive before the massive doors and stone facade, Tess Parker felt a frisson of fear snake up her spine. That, in and of itself, was terribly unnerving for her. She stiffened her spine and put her shoulders back, refusing to give in to such nonsense. After all, she prided herself on practicality and sensibleness. Those sorts of fantastical imaginings were completely foreign to her.

Taking a deep and steadying breath, she walked up to the intricately carved doors, blackened with age, and stared at the door knocker with distaste. The wolf's head was impossibly realistic, down to the ruby-red glass eyes that it contained. The ring which dangled from between its bared teeth was a snake coiled in on itself, swallowing its own tail. Grim. Unnecessarily gruesome, she thought.

"And hardly welcoming," she mused as she gingerly lifted it and let it drop, striking the plate beneath. It made only a dull thud that, to her mind, should have been indiscernible within the stone structure. However, it was only a short moment before she heard the heavy scrape of the latch on the other side. Then the door swung inward slowly with a protesting creak that could only be described as haunting. It made her shiver even as it raised gooseflesh on her skin.

Once the door had opened entirely, the butler who greeted her did little to dispel her misgivings. Tall and rail thin, the man was of an indeterminate age and had an unnatural pallor. Every vein showed beneath his skin. With sharp bone structure and no hair to speak of, he looked, well, skeletal.

"I am Miss Parker from the Darrow School," she said.

"You are expected, Miss Parker," he said in a voice that was no more than a gruff whisper. Then he stepped back, his movements oddly graceful for such long, thin limbs and he made not a sound. *Like a snake.*

It took every ounce of fortitude she possessed to step through those doors and follow that man. But she did. And then the door closed behind her with a firm snap. So firm, in fact, that it made her jump. She couldn't say what it was about him that put her off so, but had she been asked to describe him in a single word, that word would have been sinister.

"His lordship is awaiting you in the study, Miss Parker. The dowager informed him that you had been retained," the butler said. There was something in the way he'd said the word "lordship", an implied sneer that indicated he did not approve of his employer.

But Tess had no chance to ask him any questions. He turned and extended one long, thin arm with fingers that seemed to stretch on indefinitely. Like an insect of some sort. *Or a spider's legs.*

Fighting back another shiver, all the while chastising herself for letting her imagination—something that had previously never reared its ugly head—get the better of her, Tess looked at the door to which he had gestured and gave a curt nod. "Thank you, sir," she managed to murmur before moving toward that door. Like everything else in the home, it was dark. But a Tudor dwelling was not exactly known for being bright and airy. It was all dark wood and heavy fabrics, after all. The coffered ceilings and heavy beams cast shadows over everything.

Pausing to take a deep breath and to smooth her sweaty palms over the dark wool of her cloak, she finally raised one hand and knocked softly.

"Enter."

That single word was barked out. It didn't sound uncivil, but rather authoritative and succinct. Oddly calmed by that very relatable impression of her employer, she opened the door and stepped into what could only be described as a masculine sanctuary. Armchairs upholstered in rich velvets and dark leathers. A carpet in shades of burgundy and green covered parquet floors. Every wall was lined with shelves that were overflowing with leather-bound books. The furnishings were all heavy, dark pieces with thick, turned legs and brass accents. Nothing was gilded. Nothing was delicate. The art on the walls in the small amount of space not dedicated to books consisted of hunting scenes. It was a room devoted to the pursuits of men and smelled faintly of brandy and cigars. And yet, she liked it. There was a warmth to that room that she certainly had not felt when viewing the exterior of the home. Had any warmth been present in the entryway, the gaunt and terrifying butler would certainly have dispelled it quickly enough.

Her gaze fell on the man at the desk. He sat hunched forward over a ledger; his impossibly dark hair was too long and concealed his face from view entirely. She had the impression of youth though—not that he was a child, but rather that he was a man in his prime. The breadth of his shoulders and the way his long legs stretched out beneath the desk, his booted feet crossed, seemed to indicate that. She felt another frisson of some unfamiliar sensation that was most decidedly not fear.

"Good afternoon, my lord. I am Miss Tess Parker from the Darrow School. Your grandmother has retained me to act as her companion."

He raised his head then, his piercing eyes beneath dark, slashing brows pinned her to the spot. Then one brow arched and a single corner of his lips quirked upward in an approximation of a smile. There was a thin, white scar high on his cheekbone, just below his left eye.

"Against my wishes," he muttered. But then he continued, "Good afternoon, Miss Parker. You arrived earlier than anticipated. By an entire day, no less."

"I am a heartier traveler than many," she said with no small amount of pride. "I took the mail coach as far as I could, then utilized a hired coach for the remainder of the journey. I understood that, given your grandmother's state of health, experience was necessary."

If he thought her unorthodox method of travel scandalous or odd, his expression did not give it away. He simply nodded. "Let us be clear. I did not wish to have a companion for my grandmother. That is a notion entirely her own. I prefer my house to be orderly, to be regimented and to have a degree of familiarity with all its inhabitants. In short, I dislike strangers. Be that as it may, I will concede to her wishes on the matter. Please sit and we will discuss the particulars of your compensation."

Tess was surprised at her reluctance. He had not been unpleasant, just shockingly forthright. He had not looked at her in that way other men had in the past—the way that left her feeling terribly uncomfortable and questioning their motives. And yet, she did not want to be closer to him. Not because she feared him, either, though he did cut a formidable figure. It was almost a premonition—a sense that if she stepped closer to him it would alter things in a way she was not prepared for.

Mentally castigating herself for such foolishness, Tess forced her feet to move, to take the few steps toward the leather chair that was closest to his desk. But with each step, the fine details of the man before her became more apparent. The shadow of beard that high-lighted the squareness of his chin and chiseled line of his jaw. It allowed her to see the way the dim light glinted off his high cheek-bones that were sharper than knife blades. And it showed, in stark relief, that unusual scar that kept his face from being simply beautiful and made it something infinitely more dangerous—it made it interest-

4

ing, it hinted at stories to be told and secrets to be revealed. In short, it made him the one thing she'd never been able to resist in her life. It made him a mystery while hinting at hidden danger. It made him the worst possible thing for her... *irresistible*.

Chapter Two

MAXIMILLIAN NIGHTLEIGH, EARL of Finmore, stared at the young woman with a sense of trepidation. When his grandmother had informed him that she had obtained a companion through the Darrow School, he had anticipated someone plain and unappealing, or rather he had hoped for such an outcome. He did not need the distraction of an attractive young woman under his roof.

Another glance at Miss Parker with her winsome face and entirely too curvaceous form had him thinking. Not attractive. Beautiful. Beguiling, even. With her auburn hair, smattering of freckles and wide green eyes, Tess Parker made him think of mermaids and sirens. She was the sort of woman who could lure a man, quite happily, to his death. *Bloody nuisance.*

What could he do? Sending her back was not an option as he had not been the one to retain her. If he didn't pay her wages and welcome her, his grandmother would just invite someone else. Miss Parker, despite her unfortunate attractiveness, at least appeared to be a sensible creature.

Cursing his luck, he managed to withhold his sigh of irritation. It wasn't her fault, after all. She could hardly be blamed for the fact that the symmetry of her features appealed to him. He did not dare to consider the rest of her. Looking at anything beyond her face was more temptation than any man should willingly torment himself with.

Keeping his tone abrupt and businesslike, he stated, "Miss Parker, my grandmother is actually in the best of health. She would have you believe that she hovers at death's door, but it is all an act designed to garner sympathy and attention."

"I understand, my lord. I had an inkling of that from the letters we exchanged prior to accepting the position. But as I see it, a woman of her age is entitled to demand a bit of sympathy and attention," she replied smoothly.

"Quite right," he agreed. "So long as you keep that in mind, I think things will go quite well. I must warn you that Nightleigh House, given its appearance and its isolation, tends to take a toll on people rather quickly. Should you elect to leave before your tenure is up—it was three months, I believe?"

"Yes, my lord, three months," she concurred.

"Naturally, you will be compensated for a period of no less than those three months, regardless of how long you must stay. If you choose to stay on after the three months, then you will be compensated monthly from that point forward."

"Your generosity is greatly appreciated, my lord."

Maxim nodded. "Do not let her manipulate you too much. She enjoys nothing more than appearing weak and sickly while meddling in people's lives."

"Are there indoor activities that your grandmother enjoys? Aside from meddling that is. I'd like to be prepared for when I meet her."

He shrugged. "You may help her with her embroidery if she chooses. Read to her. Play music for her. There is a spinet in her sitting room. In short, keep her entertained. Her health is quite robust given her age, but she is approaching eighty and there are limits to what she can do. I visit her for an hour every evening before dinner so you will have some time to yourself each day. You will have a half-day on Saturdays and you may take Sunday mornings to attend the local church if you desire."

"Again, you are very generous."

Those demure responses, her head ducked and her eyes downcast—there was something false about them. She was not the meek sort. It was all an act. But given what horrors lurked within the walls of Nightleigh House, perhaps not being a meek sort would be to her benefit. Electing to simply let the matter go, he continued, "I will have Calvert, our butler, show you to your chamber. For the sake of expedience, you've been assigned the room next to my grandmother's in the family wing rather than being put in the servants' quarters or one of the guest chambers. Your bags?"

"They are outside the front door. They are rather heavy and the coachman was not inclined to provide assistance," she admitted ruefully. "I brought some of my favorite books with me to share with your grandmother."

"Excellent," he said, sparing a glance at his own shelves. "No doubt they will be more to her taste than these dusty tomes. I'll send for the footmen to take them to your chamber."

"Excellent, thank you." She rose and turned to walk away.

"Miss Parker," he called out. When she glanced back at him over her shoulder, a classically seductive pose that women had employed for ages, he knew it wasn't intentional. That did not make it any less potent. But he hadn't halted her to simply stare at her lovely face or the elegant lines of her figure draped in her drab gown. He needed to warn her—to protect her as much as he could. "In the evenings, Miss Parker, I would suggest you remain close to your chamber or to my grandmother's."

"Does she typically require more assistance in the evenings?" the young woman asked with concern.

Maxim considered lying. It would be easier. But he couldn't bring himself to. Instead, he told a half-truth. "Not particularly, no. But this is a very old house and much of it is unsafe… especially in the dark."

"I see. And will I be given a tour to know which areas of the house are safe and which are not?" she asked.

Maxim knew that it was a reasonable request. But there was no one in the household he trusted to do so. It would have to be him. And that would mean more time in her company. It was a bloody nightmare. "Of course. When I've gotten some of this correspondence cleared away, I shall escort you myself. In the meantime, seek out Calvert. He's no doubt lurking just beyond the door."

She frowned at that description. "Lurking?"

"Figuratively, of course," he lied. He had little doubt that Calvert had been pressing a glass to the door to hear every last word exchanged. "I shall see you shortly, Miss Parker, for your tour."

<hr />

Tess rose and, offering her thanks once more, made for the door. When she opened it, she found the butler was, indeed, lurking, as his lordship had posited. The man stood only a foot from the door and there was little doubt that he'd had his ear pressed to it the entire time she'd been speaking with her employer.

"Mr. Calvert?"

"Yes, Miss Parker?"

"Would you show me to my room, please?"

"This way, Miss Parker," he said in that strange, gravelly whisper.

Tess followed the man up the stairs. They were uneven, worn down in the center from centuries of feet landing upon them. Each tread dipped in the center and pitched slightly forward, making them terrifyingly precarious. Placing her feet cautiously on each one to avoid tripping, she felt a moment of relief when they reached the upper floor. It was short-lived. A glance at the corridor and she longed to run back down those hazardous stairs and straight back to London.

The walls were paneled in wood so dark it was almost black. Sconces had been placed at regular intervals, but they did little to brighten the space. The deep red carpet that ran down the center was like a rivulet of blood. The coffered ceiling above was painted red with more of that dark wood, and each juncture of the coffers was punctuated with a finial. In all, it had the effect of making her feel like she was walking into the gaping mouth of a predator, its sharp teeth poised above her, ready to snap closed and swallow her whole. Each end of the corridor was shrouded in darkness, seeming to stretch on forever.

Calvert apparently did not have her sense of foreboding. He shuffled down the corridor as if it were nothing, leaving her to follow behind him or stand rooted to the spot—alone. Not that he provided any real sense of safety, but she found herself reluctant to be alone there. Tess fell in step behind him. They walked almost to the end of the corridor before he stopped.

"This is your chamber, Miss Parker. The dowager's chamber is next door," he said, pointing with one long, bony finger toward the door next to hers. "Dinner will be served promptly at seven. You will take your meals in the dining room as you are not quite a servant. Do you require the assistance of a maid to help you?"

The question, as posed, should have been a friendly and welcoming one. But Tess had the feeling that it was not. It felt like a test, she thought. As if the manner in which she responded would inform the butler on how she should be treated going forward. Regardless of what answer he wanted her to give, Tess had no intention of changing the way she did things. Being waited upon was not something she was accustomed to.

"No, thank you, Mr. Calvert. I will be perfectly fine on my own."

The older man smirked for just a second. "Of course, you will, Miss Parker."

With that, he turned on his heel and shuffled away, leaving her in that corridor to shiver alone. Shaking off her discomfiture, Tess stepped toward her chamber door and curled her fingers about the door handle. As she did so, she felt that same frisson of awareness that she had as she'd looked up at the house outside. It was an overwhelming sensation of not being quite alone. Daring a glance over her shoulder, she saw nothing. No movement. No shadows. And yet she felt a cool gust of air move slowly past her cheek. Too slowly to be the wind, even if there had been a single window for such a breeze to drift through. Then the door across the corridor opened slowly, the knob turning before her eyes, before the door swung inward. But there was no one there. It was simply an empty room, the furniture all covered with dust cloths.

With a soft squawk of alarm, Tess dove through the opened door of her own chamber and closed it behind her with a firm snap. She leaned against it for a moment, her breath coming in rapid pants as she tried to simply reason away the stubborn fear that had been her constant companion from the moment she disembarked her carriage.

Nightleigh House, it seemed, was full of secrets.

Chapter Three

MAXIM ENTERED HIS grandmother's chambers and immediately stopped. The sound of voices had startled him. He had not anticipated that Miss Parker would have begun her duties so quickly. Still, he was grateful for it. His grandmother was alone. She'd given up London and come with him to the desolate wilds of Cumbria when he'd inherited the title and the shambles his uncle had left behind. He knew she was lonely.

But it wasn't his relief that halted his steps. No. It was her voice. Soft, slightly husky, utterly feminine and completely entrancing. It was the voice of a seductress. And yet it belonged to a perfectly respectable young woman who was there as his employee. In short, for the sake of his honor, she was utterly forbidden to him.

When the conversation in the bedchamber fell into a lull, an indication that they were aware of his presence, he then stepped forward. Leaving the sitting room, he entered his grandmother's room and instantly smiled to see her sitting up in the bed. She had color in her cheeks and appeared quite pleased with Miss Parker.

"Good evening, Grandmother," he said softly as he approached the bed and leaned down to kiss her cheek.

She beamed at him. "Maxim! My sweet boy. So handsome. Isn't he handsome, Miss Parker?"

"It would be highly inappropriate for Miss Parker to answer that question. It is even more inappropriate for you to have asked it," he cut in, saving the companion from having to navigate such murky waters. Still, a part of him wondered. Did she find him handsome? He certainly found her beautiful even if it was damned inconvenient.

Miss Parker rose from her chair, closed her book firmly and placed it on the table next to her. "On that note, my lord, my lady, I shall take my leave and prepare for dinner."

Maxim watched her depart and then turned back to his grandmother who was smirking at him. "Stop it."

"Stop what?" she asked, the very picture of beatific innocence.

He favored his grandmother with an arched brow and a stern look. "Miss Parker is here as an employee. You retained her to be your companion. That is all. Whatever notions you have in your head about playing matchmaker, you may stop it... instantly. I will not be taking a wife as you well know... ever. And I have no intention of being the sort of cad who takes advantage of a young woman in my employ."

His grandmother waved her hand dismissively. "It's only taking advantage if your intentions are wicked. Are they wicked, Maxim?"

Crossing his arms over his chest, he didn't answer. That, in and of itself, was answer enough for her. His grandmother smiled triumphantly.

Her voice was almost girlish and giddy as she continued. "You must admit that she is exceptionally attractive. Companions, as a rule, Maxim, do not look like that. I've certainly encountered enough of them to know. Will she last, do you think? Or will this cursed place get the better of her?"

For his own sake, he rather hoped that it would. But for his grandmother's, he wondered if perhaps Miss Parker's presence might truly be of benefit to her. "On that point, I simply cannot hazard a guess. She seems to be of an imminently practical nature. That will help, I think."

"Until it grows dark. Practicality fades, dear boy, when the night closes in around you and the winds begin to howl. That is when this house is at its most vicious," she mused. "I do hope she's made of sterner stuff than some we know."

"Do not," he warned.

"Do not what?"

"I will not speak of Elizabeth. Our betrothal has ended and I have wished her well in her new life," he said. "Do not bring it up again." His former betrothed had visited Nightleigh House one time and one time only. She'd screamed about ghosts and demons before leaving the house in tears and refusing to ever set foot in it again. He did not blame her for it.

His grandmother sighed, but then smiled. "I do like her, Maxim. I like her very much. I hope that she can withstand the rigors of this house."

It would solve all of his problems if she could not, and yet, he couldn't deny a flare of hope himself. He wanted her to be spared all of it. An overwhelming feeling of protectiveness stirred in him at that moment. He wanted to save Miss Parker from the torment that Nightleigh House visited on so many. But he hadn't even managed to save himself from it.

IN HER OWN chamber, one far finer than someone of her station would typically be assigned, Tess dressed with care. Dining with Lord Finmore had created a sense of anticipation in her, unwise though it might be. She could not suppress the thrill of excitement she felt at the notion of spending so much time in his company.

Recalling the slightly goading and mischievous question from his grandmother about whether or not she found him handsome, she could feel her cheeks flushing with embarrassment. She did find him handsome. Far too handsome for her peace of mind.

Smoothing the peacock blue silk of her gown, she marveled at the texture of the fabric. The gown had been a gift from Effie, one that she had initially resisted. But Effie had insisted, reminding her that she was not going to Nightleigh House to be a governess but to be a companion. As such, she might be called upon to take part in social gatherings. Being appropriately dressed was simply a part of her duties.

Vanity prompted another pass before the large mirror. Turning to face it, she felt a stirring of pride. She looked far more than simply presentable. Leaning in to smooth any stray strand of hair from her simple but elegant coiffure, Tess turned her head slightly just to make sure that the back was smooth as well. Tilting her head to the side for a better view, her eyes went wide and the scream that wanted so desperately to escape her simply froze in her throat.

There in the reflection, standing only feet behind her, was a woman. She wore a dingy nightrail that might once have been white but was now gray with age and dirt. It was ragged and worn. Her dark hair hung over her shoulders in a tangled mass. Her head was bent forward, her face concealed entirely by the fall of her snarled hair. She made no sound. In fact, the room was so eerily quiet that Tess' skin prickled with unease.

Needing confirmation, not to mention that she felt terribly vulnerable with her back to a stranger who had wandered soundless into her chamber, Tess whirled around to face the room. But it was completely empty. There was nothing. No ragged-looking woman—nothing at all. But the room felt different. It felt cold. It felt menacing.

With a strange foreboding, she glanced behind her at the mirror. Again, it was just the reflection of the room. There was nothing there that should not be. And yet, that only intensified her fear. The hair at the nape of her neck raised in alarm and her heart was pounding violently in her chest.

A knock at her door made her jump, another shriek escaping her.

She stared at the door almost as if it might bite her. She glanced at the mirror once more.

"It was my imagination," she whispered to the empty room. With more conviction, she continued, almost as if she could speak it into truth. "The shock of being in a new place after the exhaustion of such an arduous journey has me jumping at shadows and seeing things that simply are not there. I will not let my mind play tricks on me just because this house lends itself to such dark imaginings."

Crossing to the door, she forced herself to open it despite any ridiculous fantasies about what might await her on the other side of it. With a deep breath, she grasped the handle and opened it, peering out into the corridor.

"Miss Parker? Are you well?"

It was the earl. Of course, he had been next door in his grandmother's chamber. He would have heard her. Humiliated by her own fanciful imaginings and that she'd been on the verge of hysteria for no good reason, Tess replied, "I'm quite well, my lord. My apologies if I worried you. I tripped on the rug."

He frowned at her, his expression obviously skeptical. "You're certain that is all?"

"Quite certain. New places and unfamiliar surroundings are a challenge for my natural predilection to clumsiness, I'm afraid." She offered the lie with a tight smile.

He appeared to accept the explanation, albeit with a slightly dubious expression. "In that case, allow me to offer you my escort down to dinner. The stairs can often be treacherous—even for those who are familiar with them."

Tess looked at his proffered arm. She was reluctant to touch him. It wasn't fear, loathing or any notion that perhaps he might not behave as a gentleman. It was the same sensation that had overtaken her in his study—a knowing—that it would change things.

With no reasonable excuse to refuse, Tess took a deep breath and placed her hand on his forearm. Even that simple touch was like a bolt of lightning. That point of contact sent a current arcing through her. It made her feel alive. Her skin tingled, her heart raced. It also terrified her... because she knew in that instant what it was. Desire. Never before experienced but often observed, she understood it only too well. Hesitantly, she looked up and met his gaze. It was heated, focused on her mouth with a hunger that was easily recognizable. *He felt it, too.*

"I will be fine, my lord. I would hate to be responsible for both of us tumbling down the stairs," she said, withdrawing her hand from his arm.

"As you wish," he conceded.

Without the warmth and firmness of his muscular arm beneath her hand, she felt strangely bereft. The man was dangerous to her. He sparked something inside her that she was not at all comfortable with. It was something she had managed to avoid in her life, a complication that only ever led to disaster. Now, she was hundreds of miles from London with no escape in sight and the character flaw that every female in her family had succumbed to—wantonness—had suddenly manifested in her. It was a disaster.

"Are you certain you are well, Miss Parker?"

Realizing that she must have made some sound of distress, Tess looked up into his face, now etched with concern. "Quite well, my lord. Simply contemplating the vagaries of fate."

He smirked slightly, his lips curving upward in wry amusement. "That topic will offer no definitive answers. Only never-ending frustration."

She nodded. "So it will. Perhaps we can find more pleasant matters to discuss over dinner."

"I will endeavor to try."

Chapter Four

DINNER HAD BEEN a shockingly pleasant affair. Maxim dined alone more often than not. He would occasionally take meals in his grandmother's room to keep her company or would sometimes dine with friends at a neighboring estate. But having Miss Parker in his dining room, enjoying her wit and beauty while partaking of an expertly prepared meal—it made him think of things he should not. It made him want things he should not. Elizabeth had been proof of that. As a man haunted—cursed, even—such things as marriage and a family were out of his reach.

"Tell me about Nightleigh House," Miss Parker suggested as their dessert was served. The confection of sugared fruit served over a liqueur-soaked cake was simple but delicious and one of his favorites.

"What would you like to know?" he asked somewhat cautiously. There was little enough to say that would not frighten her half to death.

"The history of it must be fascinating... I recognized the architecture as Tudor from the outside, but some of the interior's features appear to be even older," she commented.

"That is all very true. Some of the interior walls were salvaged from a sacked Saxon stronghold. They were incorporated into a thirteenth-century fortress that was built on the site. Then, through all the various ruling houses of our glorious country, the estate changed hands numerous times. It became the property of the Nightleigh's during the reign of Henry the Seventh. A larger structure in the Tudor style was built around the existing castle, encompassing it entirely... I believe that I promised you a tour, but it's much too late tonight," he said, sticking to the most vague description of the architecture of the house while avoiding any hint of its dark history. No one strolled the corridors of Nightleigh Hall after dark, not willingly at any rate.

"Have you always lived here?" she asked.

"No. I lived primarily in London with my parents. But we summered here frequently... and after their deaths, I went away to school."

"But you spent your holidays here?"

He had been spared that horror. "No."

"Oh. I'm sorry. My questions must seem very impertinent."

Realizing that he'd been more abrupt than he'd intended, Maxim shook his head. "Not at all, Miss Parker. I've simply forgotten how to make polite conversation. Forgive me. As to the estate, alas, my uncle passed away without an heir and now it has come to me to take on the earldom. For better or worse."

Miss Parker put down her fork, the cake before her only half-eaten.

"Is it not to your liking?"

She looked up in surprise. "On the contrary. It's quite delicious. But if I have any hope of continuing to fit into the wardrobe I have brought with me, I will have to curb my inclination to gluttony."

Thinking too much about the figure concealed beneath her very fetching gown was a disaster waiting to happen. But it was either that or be consumed with the other thought her comment had sparked. Maxim was suddenly terribly curious about which of the remaining deadly sins might also be her downfall. It was wrong of him to hope that lust might top her list, but the urge was there even if his conscience prevented him from acting upon it.

Realizing that he'd been quiet for far too long, Maxim cleared his throat. "Ah, I understand. You are my grandmother's companion, Miss Parker, but you need not spend every minute in her chamber. If you wish to walk the grounds while she takes her naps, you certainly may. And if you are an experienced rider, you may certainly have access to a mount while you are here."

She nodded. "Thank you, my lord, I will certainly do that. But it was a long journey today and I find that I am very tired. Alas, I fear I may also be possessed of a poor sense of direction. Would it be possible to ring for one of the maids to show me to my chamber?"

The maids would be tucked away down in the kitchen, ready to tidy up for the night and then move en masse to the servants' quarters. They would not wander the halls alone after dark and he could not blame them. If he tried to order one to do so, the tearful and wailing protest that would be sent up would raise too many questions. "I will escort you. My own chambers are in the same wing."

"Oh... thank you," she said.

HER ENTIRE PURPOSE in ending the dinner early had been to escape the too handsome nobleman. His presence was disturbing. It robbed her of her much-needed reserve. As he'd talked, she'd felt herself leaning in to hear him, savoring the deep rumble of his voice and the way the light played over the knife-blade sharp cheekbones and the squared chin that could have been hewn from marble. But it was his icy blue eyes rimmed in thick black lashes that held her in sway. And the fullness of his lips set in stark contrast by the evening whiskers that shadowed his jaw—she could not afford to think about those. Her mind might then wander to places that were far too dangerous—like being kissed by him, like having him whisper sweet nothings against her ear. Oh, yes, the Earl of Finmore was incredibly dangerous to her. Primarily because he brought out the wicked part of her that she'd suppressed so successfully until meeting him. And now, he was going to be escorting her to her bedchamber.

Tess watched as he rose from his chair and walked around the table. The candlelight cast one side of his face in golden light while the other side, with its mysterious scar, remained in shadow. Rising from her chair, she accepted his proffered arm and they left the dining room together, heading toward the dark-paneled staircase that had created such anxiety in her before. It was still terrifying, but less so in his presence.

Climbing the treacherous steps at his side, Tess breathed a sigh of relief when they reached the top. She had managed not to trip and make an utter cake of herself. Looking down the corridor, that brief feeling of safety prompted by his presence simply vanished. The wall sconces created small pools of golden light, but they did nothing to penetrate the pockets of deep, black shadows. Those shadows seemed to writhe as the candles on the wall flickered. Like snakes, she thought. Without conscious thought, she stepped closer to him. So close, in fact, that her shoulder brushed against his chest.

Startled, Tess turned her head to look up at him over her shoulder. He was gazing down at her with an inscrutable expression.

"This house, Miss Parker... it can play tricks on your mind. The floors and walls are uneven. The darkness seems to be impenetrable at times. But you are safe here," he said. "Always remember that. Nothing in this house can bring you harm... but if you allow your imagination free rein, if it prompts you to run or hide or explore places that are unsafe—that, Miss Parker, is what I cannot protect you from. Do you understand?"

Tess did understand. It was not her imagination. What she had seen in her room had been real. The writhing shadows along the corridor—they were real, too. They could not hurt her, but her fear could lead her to hurt herself. "Yes, my lord. I think I understand perfectly."

"Good," he said, then walked her down the corridor while keeping his eyes firmly straight ahead. He never glanced to one side or the other. And if there were strange sounds that followed them, if the shadows shifted and moved around them in a way that she could not think of as natural, he ignored it.

Tess followed his example and found herself safely deposited outside her chamber door. "Thank you, my lord."

"Goodnight, Miss Parker."

Tess opened the door. But before she could step over the threshold, she saw his hand come and press against the door frame, halting any forward motion from her. Against the dark, carved wood, his hand looked impossibly strong and painfully masculine. For a moment, she wondered what it would feel like to have him touch her, to feel those strong, elegant fingers moving over her skin.

Tess turned to face him. But she was far closer to him than she'd realized. In fact, she was now fully encircled by his arm and the door at her back. His face was only scant inches from hers. The dim light from her room cast the planes and angles of his face in harsh shadows.

Neither of them spoke. For the longest moment, they remained there in complete silence, their proximity to one another creating a potent awareness. Then he leaned in, just close enough that his mouth hovered next to her ear. His breath fanned over that delicate skin and she shivered in response. But it wasn't a sweet nothing that he whispered to her.

"Miss Parker... whatever you may hear or see, do not leave your room at night. Promise me that."

"Yes, my lord," she said breathlessly. "I promise."

It might have been an accident. Or it could have been simply her own wishful imaginings, but she felt the tender brush of his lips over her cheek as he pulled back. Then he nodded and his hand fell away from the door frame. He turned to vanish into the darkness of the corridor.

Tess, feeling far more frightened than she ever had—of the house and its secrets and of her own wicked urges—ducked into her room. With shaking hands, she closed the door behind her. It was a foolish impulse, especially as she'd already learned that she was not safe even in her own chamber, but she locked the door regardless. Then she leaned back against the wood and tried desperately to catch her breath and to still the racing of her heart that had only a small amount to do with the dark goings-on of Nightleigh House.

Chapter Five

I T WAS THE middle of the afternoon. The dowager was napping after a rousing card game and several chapters of a particularly lurid gothic novel. Tess could feel herself blushing as she recalled reading certain passages of it aloud. The dowager, however, had howled with delight. In short, she was the least dowager-like dowager that Tess could even begin to imagine. They'd played cards after, and Tess had been thoroughly routed.

Rather than remain in the house, with its air of palpable menace and terrifying secrets, *and its mysterious and oh-so-tempting master,* she'd elected to go outside. Walking the grounds, bundled in her warm pelisse, she'd enjoyed the scenery despite the colder temperatures. It was a place of contrasts. Mountains rose in the distance to the north, sharp and jagged. To the east, long flat fields of green grass dotted with large stones rolled gently toward the sea. The sea was a thing of anger on that day—gray and moody, the depths of it roiling up in white-capped waves that surely would have capsized any vessel unwary enough to challenge them. To the south, the land sloped sharply, the lane bisecting heavy trees to lead into the village. And to the west, behind her, was the dark, hulking shape of Nightleigh House. She felt its long shadow falling over her even as the rain threatened. Wearing only her spencer with no heavy cloak to protect her, she had no choice but to return.

A glance over her shoulder and she could see dark clouds looming above its gabled roof. Yes, getting away from it for a short while had been the right decision. It had given her some perspective and, she hoped, an opportunity to brace herself for whatever was to come. There was something wrong at Nightleigh House—something dark and sinister. Possibly something unnatural. She'd been awakened in the middle of the night by a terrible scratching noise. It had seemed to come from within the walls itself. Not rats. Of that, she was certain. No rat could make that sound. And in the darkness, she'd felt the weight of a menacing gaze. That experience still weighed heavily upon her as she turned to face what was to come.

Climbing the slight incline back to the house, she felt her feet dragging as she moved closer and closer to it. She couldn't suppress a shiver as she opened the door and stepped inside. The oppressiveness of it seemed to settle deep in her bones, heavy and dreadful as the darkness of it closed around her.

Calvert was nowhere to be seen. The man unnerved her, always hovering nearby, observing and listening with an interest that went far beyond simply being a good servant. She'd seen him as she'd left the house, watching her with suspicion and no small degree of animosity. But Tess was reluctant to simply return to her room, and as the dowager was still sleeping, she had no other options. The earl had made himself scarce since dinner the night before, so she still had no notion which areas of the house were safe for her to enter or not. If any area of Nightleigh House could be considered safe!

As if her thoughts had summoned him, a door at the end of the corridor opened and the earl appeared. He wore breeches and boots but was only in shirtsleeves and his waistcoat. His coat and cravat had been discarded somewhere along the way, if he'd bothered to don them at all. It was an all too appealing sight.

"Good afternoon, Miss Parker. My grandmother is still resting. It appears your revelries this morning have left her quite weary," he explained.

"It was her victory, my lord, that exhausted her, along with all the crowing she did afterward. I am apparently a truly terrible card player and no competition for her at all."

"As am I," he concurred. "But in the bright light of the afternoon, we have an opportunity to tour the house so that I may show you which areas are safe. There is a sitting room upstairs that you may use at your convenience. Though, I would caution you to seek the solace of your room before it grows dark in the evenings. I can show you to it, if you like."

"Thank you. That would be most appreciated, my lord."

Climbing the stairs once more with him at her side, they walked down the corridor in the opposite direction from her chamber and his grandmother's. He opened one of the doors to show her into a small sitting room. It was decorated in lighter tones than many other rooms in the house. The Aubusson rug was comprised of shades of cream, sea green and gold. The walls were covered in a damask wallpaper in soft green and the furniture was upholstered in a similar shade of velvet. There was a small cherry writing desk in the corner, its intricately carved legs and drawer fronts softly gilded.

"It's a lovely space," she said.

"It was my grandmother's favorite room when I was younger... before she kept mostly to her own chambers," he offered. "Come, I'll show you the rest of the house."

The tour was short. There were rooms on that floor which were not bedchambers at all. Some of the doors concealed staircases or corridors that led to other parts of the house. One staircase tucked away at the end of the corridor led to another floor that contained a large ballroom. The house was like a maze, or perhaps a rabbit warren. Now she understood why it would be utterly treacherous to go exploring on her own. She might never find her way back.

"The door directly across from mine... what is that room?" she asked.

His expression shuttered. "That room is unused, Miss Parker. There was substantial storm damage to the roof above it which has resulted in the floor being compromised. Please do not enter that chamber. In fact, the door should be locked."

"When Calvert showed me to my room yesterday, that door opened."

"It was open?" he demanded, angrily. "I have given express orders that no one is to enter it!"

"No, Lord Finmore. It *opened*. I glanced over my shoulder and that door opened in a slow, controlled manner... as if someone were opening it though I could see no one there," she admitted.

His expression became completely inscrutable, his eyes going cold and dark. "Superstitious nonsense, Miss Parker. The room is compromised and partially open to the elements. It was likely the wind."

Except there had been no wind yesterday, she thought. Suddenly, she found herself questioning whether or not the man before her could be trusted. Keeping her tone neutral, she still couldn't rally any sincerity behind her words as she replied, "Of course, Lord Finmore. No doubt it was the exhaustion of the day that prompted my mind to play tricks on me. I will see you at dinner."

"Until then, Miss Parker," he said. "Good afternoon."

MAXIM TURNED AND walked away, just managing to stop himself from glancing over his shoulder at that damnable door. His grandmother had refused to change rooms, refused to be run from her own space by what she referred to as a spiritual nuisance. For himself, it was infinitely more than that. It struck terror in his heart. It sent him hurtling back to that night of terror he'd endured as a child. He hadn't entered that room since he'd been a boy of eight years old. There likely wasn't a power on earth that could force him to do so.

Cursing under his breath even as he steadfastly ignored the prickling unease that settled between his shoulder blades, Maxim clenched his teeth. He would not be cowed. He was not a child any longer. But it was clear to him that whatever lurked within that room was toying with them, luring Miss Parker to that space.

It was using her to get him.

The certainty of that cemented for him just how much of a liability the companion was. He needed to stay away from her. He needed to keep his head and she clearly threatened his ability to do so. Determined, Maxim headed for his own chambers, a new strategy firmly in mind.

Chapter Six

T ESS STARED DOWN the expanse of the beautifully laid dinner table. The floral centerpieces and candelabras were stunning. The chandelier above glittered like the Crown Jewels. The snowy linens were pristine. And the seat at the head of the table remained empty. She dined in that space alone—surrounded by luxury that she was not entitled to, the riches of an aristocratic home spread out before the illegitimate child of a viscount's younger son and a vicar's disgraced daughter. She did not belong.

It had been one thing to dine in that beautiful, if somewhat dark and terrifying, dining room when Lord Finmore had been dining as well. Then it had simply been a matter of polite conversation. But sitting in that room alone, she felt like a fraud.

"Mr. Calvert?"

The butler stepped forward from his post near the dining room doors. "Yes, Miss Parker?"

"Is his lordship not dining tonight?"

The butler sniffed, as if he disapproved of her having the gall to ask about his lordship's whereabouts. "No, Miss Parker. He asked for a tray in his study."

Tess felt the man's disapproval keenly. He stared at her with cold disdain. "I see. In the future, if his lordship does not dine formally, I should like to be accommodated in a similar fashion. A tray in my room would suffice, or a tray sent up for me along with the dowager's. I would prefer to dine with her."

"Certainly, Miss Parker. Would you like a tray to be sent up for you tonight?"

Looking at the table again, she shook her head. "No, Mr. Calvert. Thank you. I find that I have lost my appetite... please excuse me."

Getting up from the table, Tess rushed from the dining room and made for the stairs. She wasn't certain what she had done to offend him or why she was suddenly being treated like a pariah, but she knew that he had lied to her that afternoon. *He'd lied to her about the room across the hall and now he was avoiding her.* Was it guilt? Was she afraid that she might demand the truth from him?

When she reached the top of the stairs, the corridor was much darker than she'd anticipated. The meager light from the wall sconces seemed unable to penetrate the deep shadow. And near the end of the corridor, she saw movement. Was it his lordship?

A glimmer of white seemed to beckon her. Was it a servant? His lordship in his shirt sleeves? Without even thinking of what she was doing, Tess took off in the direction of that white shape.

"Hello?" she called out.

The white shape at the end of the corridor halted. It simply stopped, allowing her to draw nearer to it. Even as she did so, the darkness in the hall seemed to become thicker, deeper. Darker. It was harder to make sense of her surroundings and to know how far she was from her own chamber. Slightly disoriented, she still pressed on. The closer she came, the more Tess realized that the figure she pursued was not simply cloaked in white. There was a mass of tangled dark hair. But it was no phantom, she argued with herself. It was a woman of flesh and blood surely.

"Are you lost?" Tess asked. She was only twenty feet or so from her. She felt a frisson of unease. Surely, she would have simply spoken to her? Was she mute? Impaired in some way?

But the woman's steps halted. And slowly, her head turned, glancing over her shoulder in Tess' direction. Terror filled Tess' heart. She'd been wrong. That was no flesh and blood woman. Where her eyes should have been were great black hollows. Her skin was as white as chalk and strangely flat... dull, as if it lacked the ability to reflect any light.

She'd never actually seen a ghost. Oh, there had been that glimpse in the mirror that she had convinced herself was nothing but her imagination. But this was no trick of the eyes. This was a waking nightmare right before her.

Frozen in her fear, Tess was rooted to the spot as it took one step toward her and then another. Then the figure began to turn fully, her white feet stark against the dark crimson of the carpets.

The panic that had been rising inside her seemed to boil over then. A scream escaped Tess and that sound seemed to unlock her body. Spinning on her heel, Tess ran. Her slippered feet were silent on the carpeted floor of the hall even as her legs pumped and she ran for all that she was worth. Her legs were pumping, her heart racing, and she dared not look over her shoulder. She didn't want to see that horrible creature behind her, she didn't want to imagine that it pursued her. Her only goal was to reach the safety of her chamber—to put a closed and locked door between herself and whatever horror it was.

But she did not reach her room. In the darkness of the corridor, she slammed into a hard form as another scream erupted from her.

>>>><<<<

MAXIM CAUGHT HER, his arms closing about her even as she pushed against his chest, struggling with all her might. He'd been halfway up the stairs when she had screamed the first time. He knew the sound of terror—recognized it well.

"Miss Parker! Miss Parker!" There was no response from her but her continued struggles.

"Tess," he said softly. "Tess, you are safe. I have you."

That gentle tone seemed to reach her. Her hands dropped from his chest and she stared up at him. White faced and shaking, her lower lip trembled and tears had gathered on her lower lashes, glistening in the dim light. As difficult as it was, he tore his gaze from her face and instead focused on the darkness beyond her. The corridor was unnaturally black, the shadows extending far beyond what they should have. He could see no form, no terrifying figure lurking there. But he had no doubt of the presence. He could feel it in the gooseflesh that raised on his skin.

Eager to be away from that unknown threat, Maxim simply scooped her into his arms and strode across the hall to the doors of his chamber. Inside, he deposited her on a settee before a roaring fire. They would be safe in his chamber, protected by the many candles and lamps that burned inside. Candles that he never permitted to go out.

"What happened?" he asked her.

"I saw... something. Someone? I cannot say," she whispered. "It was horrible. The most terrifying thing I've ever seen... and yesterday, I thought—it's not possible."

He knew that she was on the verge of hysterics. Clasping his hands on her shoulders, he forced her to look up at him. "There are things in this house that ought to be impossible but are not. But I must know what you saw... who you saw."

"A woman," she said, her voice rising with fear, "with long, black hair and great dark hollows where her eyes should have been. That was no living woman, my lord. Tell me—truthfully—are there spirits in this house?"

Maxim felt the tremors that rocked her. Sliding his hands down her arms, he clasped her small hands in his. "I should not have left you alone at dinner. I didn't think—I never imagined that you would be so sensitive to the strangeness of this house."

"Sensitive? I'm losing my mind," she said tightly, clenching her hands in her lap, the fabric of her gown bunching between her fingers.

"You are safe here. I will not let anything harm you," he promised.

"Safe? Alone in the bedchamber of a man I barely know? Safe?" she demanded incredulously.

"You are safe from anyone and anything that means you harm," he said. "But obviously, this is not an ideal solution. I could not leave you in the corridor until I knew what the threat was."

"What is it?" she asked. "It was not a woman. I know that much."

He moved away and shook his head. "It is the thing that has haunted me for all of my life... but the why of it, I cannot say. I saw her the first time when I was a boy and I have lived in fear of her since."

She blinked at him. "That is not what I expected you to say. Does it—she appear often?"

"No. None of the previous manifestations have been so bold. Not in years. You must be the key to that, Tess. But why?"

A faint scratching noise surrounded them. It seemed to come from the very walls around them. It came once. Then again. Maxim watched as Tess brought her arms up, hugging herself tightly. There were times when he'd thought he was going mad. But she saw it. She saw it and she heard it. It offered him vindication, at least, if not comfort.

"What is that?"

"Those noises are a constant companion to me. In every room of this house, I hear them... but more so here. Only grandmother's room seems to be free of them. Have you heard them in your chamber?"

"No," she said. "Not yet, at least. Are you certain this isn't some sort of elaborate hoax?"

He laughed bitterly. "What sort of hoax lasts for more than twenty years?"

She rose and walked toward him, stopping only inches from him.

When she spoke, she did so with a conviction that was in stark contrast to the gooseflesh on her skin and the pallor of her face. Bravado in the face of terror.

"I do not know. But while I was frightened in the corridor," she admitted, "that scratching in the walls is not done by a phantom. That is either some sort of vermin or it is a person. No ghost can do all of that."

He shook his head. "I have looked. I have searched this house over. If there is a flesh and blood person responsible for these things, I have found no evidence of it."

"Then we will look together," she said. "I will not live in fear and I will not let you continue to do so either."

Maxim took in the determined tilt of her chin, the stubborn set of her jaw, her shoulders back as if she were ready to march into battle. She was, in that moment, an irresistible combination of fierceness and delicacy. And he could hold back no longer. The determination he'd had to hold fast to his will and not give in to the temptation of her simply fled. Unable to help himself, Maxim reached for her, hauling her toward him with a hunger that would surely terrify her. But when his lips claimed hers, when he kissed her with all the need he felt roiling inside him, she did not back away. Instead, she met him evenly, her lips moving beneath his with equal ardor. But it was her first kiss. That much was evident in the untutored, but still enticing, way she kissed him back. Determined not to be an ass, to give more than he took, Maxim forced himself to gentle the kiss, to ease it into something that was more about seduction than raw need.

Still, the softness of her lips beneath his, the sweetness of her mouth at that first tentative taste, was more tempting than anything he'd ever encountered. So he savored and explored. He deepened the kiss, sweeping his tongue into her mouth and tasting her fully, mimicking other intimate acts that were ever-present in his mind. And, Heaven help him, she responded in kind. Innocent and untutored, but passionate and eager—it was a heady combination.

Struggling to keep his own desires in check, Maxim allowed his hands to move over her. Caressing her arms, her shoulders, skating lightly over her ribs and down to her waist. They settled there, mapping the narrow curve of her waist and the flare of her hips. It fueled his already vivid imagination. It made him long to see her spread out before him, naked and his for the taking. But that would wait. That kiss, in that moment, it was for her.

But that kiss ended in chaos. There were screams from the corridor and when Maxim broke contact with her, he turned to look back at the door and saw the faint wafts of smoke drifting beneath it. "Fire," he whispered in fear. "God above. My grandmother!"

He made for the door, pulling her with him. But when they emerged into the corridor, what had seemed to be a terrible fire now appeared to be something else altogether. A bucket had been placed in the center of the corridor, filled with rags soaked in oil; they burned and smoked, but presented no real danger—or at least no danger beyond discovery. The servants stood there gaping at them as the master of the house and his grandmother's companion emerged from his bedchamber. It had been a ruse designed to ruin her and send her packing.

Maxim's hardened gaze scanned the gathered servants, finding Calvert standing on the fringe of the group, a disapproving sneer on his face. But in the man's gaze, there was a hint of satisfaction. Turning away, he saw his grandmother in the doorway of her chamber.

"Maxim, what is the meaning of this?" she demanded.

"It's quite simple, Grandmother. I've asked Miss Parker to be my wife and she has agreed," he said, squeezing Tess' hand as he told the lie. "Once this bit of vandalism is addressed, we will celebrate it properly."

Chapter Seven

*B*ETROTHED.

After a long and sleepless night, one filled with anxious thoughts and jumping at every creak and groan of the ancient house, Tess was bleary-eyed and suffering a terrible headache when she rose.

That word—betrothed—kept running through her mind. Over and over again, she heard him making that announcement as he squeezed her hand to urge her cooperation. What could she have done but cooperate? To deny his claim would be to invite the utter destruction of her reputation. She'd be cast out—a fallen woman. The simple truth of the matter was, though it goaded her to admit it, she should be grateful to him. Very few men of his standing, a peer, would have done something so rash and heroic. Ruining a governess or companion for gentlemen was seen as a matter of course in most cases. It was both expected and accepted, to some degree.

After seeing to her morning ablutions, even while she brooded over her current situation, Tess left her room and made her way to the dowager's chamber. Though it was well past the dawn, and the day outside was bright and clear, the hallway was still dim and dark. But it was much less frightening than it had been the night before. The scent of smoke still lingered though the bucket with its burned rags had been disposed of.

Entering the dowager's room, she didn't knock. If her ladyship was still sleeping after the upsetting events of the night before, the last thing she wished to do was wake her. As Tess eased into the room, she heard a masculine voice—a very familiar one. He was there.

"What did you do, Grandmother?" he demanded. There was anger in his tone, but no heat. Whatever she'd done to incur his wrath, he'd clearly had some time to come to grips with it.

"I don't know what you mean, Maxim. Really. Stop being so cryptic," she answered breezily.

"I saw Dawson's hand," he said. "A fire was set in the corridor last night, very near your chamber and, this morning, your maid has her hand bandaged because she supposedly injured herself while helping in the kitchen? I'm many things, but foolish is not one of them."

"Dawson is a maid, Maxim. It's quite possible—"

"She's a lady's maid," he interrupted. "And servants are far greater snobs than any member of the nobility could ever hope to be. A woman who has reached the heights of being a lady's maid does not do the work of a kitchen girl, no matter the circumstances. Why? Why did you do it?"

"Because you need a wife and if left to your own devices, you would never get one," she replied.

Tess covered her mouth with her hand to keep in the squeak of surprise. She hadn't believed it at first. Why in Heaven's name would the dowager choose her to be his wife?

The old woman continued, "You spend too much time alone, Maxim. And I will not live forever. I am the last member of your family—the last. When I am gone, you will be entirely alone. When I heard Miss Parker scream last night and saw you carrying her away, I knew that it was innocent, of course. You are nothing if not honorable. But I also knew that your honor would compel you to do right by her if that misleading but still compromising situation was discovered."

"You sabotaged us both. You manipulated and managed us into a betrothal that neither of us wanted," he accused.

That was more painful to hear than she had expected. But, Tess thought grimly, if one listened at doors, one often heard unpleasant things. Before it could go any further, she knew she had to stop the conversation. Tiptoeing back to the door, she opened and closed it more loudly, calling out cheerily, "Good morning, my lady."

The conversation inside the bedchamber died away entirely as Tess approached that doorway. Stepping inside, she feigned surprise at seeing him there. "Good morning, Lord Finmore."

"Miss Parker," he acknowledged. "You slept well after the evening's excitement?"

"Quite," she lied. "You?"

"Not a wink," he admitted, staring balefully at his grandmother. "But I have much to attend to today. I need to obtain our marriage license, after all."

"I'd like to speak with you... privately—in the corridor, before you go," Tess said.

"Very well. Pardon us, Grandmother," he said and then strode toward the door.

Tess followed after him and stepped out into the hall. "You don't have to do this. We will simply feign an engagement for a suitable amount of time. After things have settled, we can call everything off. I'll go back to London and you can—well, you can do whatever it is that you wish to do. But you do not have to feel bound by honor to sacrifice everything and marry me when it is clearly the last thing you desire."

"If it were simply a matter of desire, Tess, you would already be my wife," he snapped.

"You are making no sense. You've no wish to marry me!" Tess snapped. The entire situation had gotten completely out of hand and they would be paying for it for the rest of their lives.

"I had no wish to marry anyone," he replied.

Tess gasped and wheeled to face him. "Well, that certainly bodes well, doesn't it?"

"It isn't personal, Tess. That thing you saw last night... it has tormented me since childhood. When I was here in this house, I lived in fear of seeing it every waking moment. And when I was away from here, I questioned my own sanity on a daily basis. Taking a wife when I couldn't be certain whether I was cursed or mad is hardly fair to anyone, now is it?"

"You aren't mad. I saw it, too. It's real. But what it is and what it wants—that I cannot say. I do, however, mean to find out," she insisted. "This will not continue. You cannot live this way."

"How do you mean to do that?" he fired back. "Ask the ghost? I will freely admit that I haven't the courage for that."

Tess squared her shoulders. "If I must. But I rather thought I'd begin with the servants... the ones who have been here the longest."

"That would be Calvert. I can assure you he will not be forthcoming."

She grimaced. "Of course not. Did your uncle suffer the misery of these ghostly visits?"

"I think so. He never said. He wouldn't have," Maxim replied.

"Where are his papers? In your study? Did you find a journal or any letters when you took his chamber?"

"I didn't take his chamber," Maxim admitted. "I would not. That room... it's the first place I ever saw her. I can't even bear to enter it."

And then she knew. It was the room across the corridor from hers. "Then I will."

"It isn't safe."

"I will be careful. I can search it this morning. I will not take any unnecessary risks and I will have a maid outside the door at all—"

"No! Not that room, Tess. Do not even think of it," he demanded. "Promise me."

Tess said nothing further. He would not be reasonable about it and she could see how much it would cost him to enter that room himself.

What he doesn't know will not hurt him. "Very well. I will not spend the morning searching that room."

"I will leave this afternoon to get the license... though, if you are willing, we could always head for Gretna Green. It's only a few hours' ride. We could leave in the morning."

Tess felt her heart stutter in her chest at the mere thought of it. Being his wife would—well, she could give in to all of those terrible yearnings without guilt then. But she also had her pride. "You have not actually asked me to be your wife. You have simply declared that we will wed," she pointed out. "I do still have a choice."

"Do you? Every servant in this house saw you. I might add, they have no loyalty to me. I've been here less than six months. They were all hired by my uncle in the last few years, save for my grandmother's maid who came with us from London and Calvert who has been here for the ages," he said. "They will talk. To their families. To servants at neighboring estates. In the village on their half-days. And eventually that gossip will make it to their sisters, brothers, cousins, and so on who have sought to make their fortunes in London. Secrets, Miss Parker, never remain secrets. So, in light of that, Miss Parker, will you be my wife?"

She'd known him for only three days. And yet, when she opened her mouth to speak, she said, "Yes, I will."

At her answer, his gaze flared with something she recognized only too well. The sharp need blazed in his eyes far brighter than any mere flame ever could. Abruptly, she turned away from him, reaching for the door to the dowager's chambers. Anything was better than facing him with her own wicked thoughts, making her blush.

"Miss Parker—Tess. It's utterly ridiculous to continue with such formalities under the circumstances," he said gruffly. "This does not have to be a terrible experience for either of us."

"I know that... but I also know that we could be making a terrible mistake. We know next to nothing about one another. And despite what I presume is a mutual attraction, there is no guarantee of happiness."

"There are never guarantees of happiness. Not for any couple, regardless of how well they know one another," he said, stepping closer to her. In fact, he moved so close that hardly any space separated them at all. "But perhaps that can work to our benefit."

"What does that mean?"

"It means, Tess, that from the moment you crossed the threshold of Nightleigh House, I have felt drawn to you—tempted by you. I didn't avoid having dinner with you last night because I didn't enjoy your company or because my work truly kept me away. I did so because I was attempting to avoid the unbelievable temptation that you present. Now, that avoidance ends. Now, we make a choice, Tess, to know one another—to trust one another—and to build something together that could, if we let it, make both of us very happy."

MAXIM WATCHED HER intently. She blushed prettily and turned her face away, refusing to answer his question. God above, but she was lovely. He had not been so tempted by a woman in all of his life. Had it not been for his grandmother's interference, that single kiss from the night before would have been the end of it. Whatever it would have taken, he would have preserved her honor—even at the sake of his own sanity. But now, with the prospect of marriage looming ahead of them, he felt a sense of possessiveness for her that had not been there before. He looked at her and thought, with a sort of primal satisfaction, *mine.*

The corridor was deserted, the servants having long since taken care of their morning duties above stairs. Alone, with the faint light filtering in at either end of the hall and the lingering scent of smoke hovering about them, it was hardly a romantic setting. And yet romance was very much on his mind. She looked up at him then, her gaze lingering on his lips, before she lowered her gaze. The tip of her tongue moved over her lower lip in such a way that it gave rise to a hundred carnal thoughts that all raced through his mind.

Unable to resist the temptation of it, Maxim leaned in and kissed her soundly. He claimed her mouth with all the hunger and need that burned inside him. That she met his ardor equally did nothing to abate the need he felt for her. Within seconds, the kiss had grown into something else, altering and shifting into a thing that had a life of its own. When he pressed her against the wall, her breasts crushed against his chest, she moaned into his mouth and he nearly lost his mind. And when he reached down, hooking his hands beneath her thighs and lifting her up, she welcomed him between them, allowing him to feel the heat of her against him. Even through their layers of clothes, that fire blazed out of control.

Tearing his lips away from hers, he trailed kisses along the tender column of her neck, nipping at a particular sensitive spot just below her ear. "You drive me mad," he murmured. "No woman has ever made me this way."

"It's a madness that has taken us both," she answered breathlessly, even as her fingers clutched at his shoulders, her nails digging into him as if she never meant to let go.

He wanted her naked. He wanted to strip away every barrier and kiss every last inch of her. Lifting her away from the wall, he turned, intending to take her straight to his room and do just that. But the sight that greeted him would effectively cool anyone's ardor. Calvert stood there, disapproval and disdain clearly evident on his face.

"My lord, the solicitor is here to see you. Apparently, there are documents that require your signature."

There was no dignified way to extricate them from the situation. "I will be there shortly."

"Yes, my lord," the butler said, still glaring at Tess.

"That will be all, Calvert," Maxim stated pointedly.

Another glare and the butler turned slowly on his heel and walked away.

"As far as humiliation is concerned, I'd have to say that mine is now thoroughly and ruthlessly complete," Tess said. "You may put me down."

"I really do not want to," he replied. "But if I don't, no doubt Calvert will simply bring the solicitor up here."

"Go. See to your business. I will spend the rest of the morning with your grandmother."

Reluctantly and with a terrible pang of regret, Maxim eased her feet back to the floor, steadying her as she regained her balance. They stood there for a moment, leaning against one another, both of them more than a bit rocked by the intensity of what had just passed between them.

"This is not over," he said. "Tonight, Tess, we will be revisiting this."

She looked up at him, a cheeky smile tugging at her lips. "I certainly hope so. It would be a shame for me to break family tradition and not be thoroughly disgraced before my wedding."

Maxim was grinning as he walked away. That grin faded the moment he stepped foot on the stairs. Calvert was waiting for him halfway down the steps, like he was a recalcitrant child who might need prodding.

"My lord, if I may be so bold, Miss Parker's behavior leaves something to be desired. While the situation last night was unfortunate, it hardly necessitates marriage. After all, it isn't as if she is a lady. Your uncle understood that not every woman a man dallies with is worthy of being a wife," the butler explained.

"As he never managed to get himself a wife, Calvert, I think he's hardly the example to live up to," Maxim retorted.

The butler's lips twisted in a sneer of disgust. "I am aware of what the Darrow School is, my lord. I know the sort of girls that are sent—"

Maxim's temper exploded then. "Enough!" His voice thundered, echoing throughout the lower floor of the house. The butler simply stared at him, hardly chastened. "Calvert, I should remind you that as soon as it can be arranged, Miss Parker will be the Countess of Finmore. You might wish to school your expressions to something that reflects a bit more passivity... and if you ever speak of her in such a manner again, they may well be the last words you ever utter."

Chapter Eight

TESS WAITED PATIENTLY. The moment the ormolu clock on the mantel showed that it was a minute past noon, she rose and left her chamber. The dowager was already napping, apparently exhausted from her machinations the night before. Maxim was still downstairs with the solicitor and she was being presented with the perfect opportunity.

Easing her door open, she peered out, checking the corridor for any potential witnesses. Seeing no one, she crept across the hall to the door of the forbidden room. Her fingers closed over the door handle and she felt her heart thundering in her chest. It was more than just the fear of getting caught. That room, and whatever lurked inside it, terrified her. But if they were to have any sort of freedom from the constant terror that stalked them at Nightleigh House, she would have to discover whatever secrets she could.

Taking a deep breath to still her trembling, she slowly turned the handle. Despite Maxim's assurance that the door was to be locked at all times, it turned easily. The door swung inward and the musty smell of rotting wood, dust and dampness assailed her. But there was nothing beyond that to immediately give her pause. It was, at first glance, just a room. Unused and in a state of disrepair, but just a room.

Stepping over the threshold, she shivered. The room was damp and cold. No fires had been lit in that fireplace in ages it seemed. When had the former earl died? Maxim had said he'd only been in residence for six months. She would need to ask him more about that. But first, she needed to find evidence of who their spirit might be and what, if anything, she had to do with Maxim's uncle.

Easing deeper into the room, she felt the floor shift beneath her feet. The wood was impossibly soft. From that point, she tested each step, placing her foot carefully as she made her way to the large armoire in the corner. It was a strange room for the lord of the manor. It was not grand, but was remarkably similar to her own room. Puzzled, she wondered what would have prompted him to use what surely had been a guest chamber.

Tess had just reached the armoire when the door to the room suddenly slammed closed behind her. With a start she looked up. It wasn't the spirit she saw standing inside that door. It was Calvert.

"What are you doing in here?" he demanded. "This room is forbidden!"

"I want to find out who she is," Tess said.

"Whom are you referring to?"

"The ghost, Mr. Calvert. I know you've seen her. You see everything here," Tess said.

The man's expression hardened. No mean feat given that he was already quite angry. "Superstitious nonsense. You must leave this room at once."

"It isn't. I saw her. With my own eyes... and Maxim is tormented by her. Has been since his childhood. Who is she? I know that you know."

At her words, Calvert flinched. "You know nothing."

His reaction was confirmation for her. He did know her identity and she was fairly certain he knew what had happened to her. "Did Maxim's uncle kill her? Did you?"

Calvert's eyes narrowed. "What do you know?"

She hadn't known anything. Not until that moment. Now it became very clear to her that she had more to fear from the butler than just his dislike of her. "You did. You did kill her!"

"No, I did not... but I brought her here. Like I brought a dozen other girls here for him to abuse. It was the only way to keep the house staffed with maids! And when he flew into a rage because she fought him, he murdered her. And I helped him hide her," Calvert admitted. "There's no proof of it in this room. I destroyed it as soon as he died. His body wasn't even cold when I tossed his journals and letters into the fire."

"Who is she?"

"Some girl from the village... I can't even remember her name," Calvert sneered. "They were happy enough to come here. Happy enough to be offered a fortune to sleep with him... until they saw him. He'd contracted the pox, you see? It was driving him mad. Making him violent and filled with rage even as it destroyed his face, eating away at the features that had once been called so handsome."

"Why would you protect him?"

"I wasn't protecting him. I was protecting myself... I brought her here. He was an earl. Beyond the reach of the law. And yet I, his half-brother, could swing for the crime he committed. So, I lied. I disposed of the body. I fired all the servants who might know or even suspect."

"Where is her body?"

Calvert shook his head. "There are a thousand places in this house to hide one. Did you know that? That's why he moved to this room. He couldn't stand to hear her scratching at night... every night. She scratches inside those walls. Then she wanders these corridors. But no one will ever find her. That hole is sealed up tight."

"He was ill. He was a monster, but he was ill—his mind destroyed by the disease... you are so much worse. You, Mr. Calvert, are evil incarnate. All those women you brought here to service him were being given a death sentence by you."

"And now you've been given one," he said. "I can't let you destroy everything. I was his half-brother. And I worked in this house... under the watchful eye of our father. He was a cruel bastard. I had my ears boxed by him more than you can imagine, for nothing more than having the audacity to exist. My mother was a whore just like the women I brought to him. Just like you are."

Tess had known when he confessed that he had no intention of letting her live. That was why she had been carefully easing back, stepping one careful inch at a time toward the dressing table that was still covered with the former earl's personal effects... including a shaving kit. If the razor was still inside it, she might have a chance.

When Calvert lunged forward, she jumped back. Her hand closed over the kit, and she struggled to open it even as he regrouped and grabbed at her. The items all tumbled out of it, falling to the floor. The razor gleamed there, bright and clean in the dull, dingy room.

His arms closed around her like steel bands. Her initial impression of him, that he was old and frail—that had clearly been a ruse on his part. The man was far stronger and much more spry than he had let on. Struggling against him, Tess brought her arm forward and then slammed her elbow back into his ribs. He gasped and, coughing fitfully, his grasp on her eased for just a moment. She dropped to her knees to grab the razor, but he must have recognized her intent. When she whirled on him, he simply ran at her, thrusting his shoulder into her stomach so that it robbed her of breath. And then the floor beneath them simply gave way.

Tess looked down as they dangled from the broken floor. They were in the part of the house that was cantilevered over the first floor so there was nothing below the but hard, rocky ground that sloped away from the house. It was a drop of at least thirty feet. Enough that if they fell, they would be gravely injured at the least... or fatally injured.

Even as she thought it, he was reaching for her hands that gripped the broken boards, prying at her fingers. So Tess did the only thing she could, she screamed for all that she was worth.

MAXIM WAS IN his study, but he was not working. The account books that were in such terrible disarray from his uncle's poor management would simply have to wait. He didn't have the patience or the concentration to tackle them at the moment. His mind was engaged elsewhere—primarily with his betrothed. The heated moments in the corridor plagued his memory. They left him yearning for more and eager for the night to come.

A sound in the distance caught his attention. It sounded wrong, somehow—out of place. It wasn't the call of a bird, or if it was, he'd never heard it before. Opening the large window, he was instantly blasted by the cold. But the sound was much louder now and there was no mistaking it. It was a woman's scream.

Climbing through the window, he stepped outside and walked to the end of the building. He heard it again and, this time, he was near enough to pinpoint the direction. He looked up and fear hit him solidly in the gut, robbing him of breath. From the upper floor, where the it cantilevered over the first, he could see legs dangling—two sets, a pair of feminine legs and the skirt of a familiar drab dress along with a pair of thin, spidery masculine legs, which he also immediately recognized.

Tess and Calvert were clinging to the rotten boards of what remained of his uncle's chamber. It would take a miracle for anyone to survive that fall.

That thought prompted him to act. He turned, ran back to the window and into the house. From there, he raced toward the stairs, praying he would get there in time.

As he cleared the stairs, he turned and felt his blood run cold. Just outside the door to that room, he saw her. The ghost. The nightmare of his childhood in stark relief. He'd never seen her in daylight before. It had always been in the dark, in the night when everything was more terrifying. She pointed toward that room, the dark hollows of her eyes seeming more sad now than monstrous.

Save her.

The words weren't spoken aloud, but they belonged to her. They whispered through his mind, raising shivers through his body. But they also pushed him to act. He raced ahead, ignoring the ghostly figure, and entered that room. What he saw made his blood run cold. Calvert, clinging to the boards with one hand, was systematically attempting to pry Tess' fingers loose where she gripped one broken joist.

"Stop!" Maxim shouted. "Calvert—do not hurt her. If you hurt her, there will be no place on earth where you can hide."

The aging butler looked at him then, his eyes blazing with hatred. And then, with a wicked twist of his mouth that might have passed for a grim smile, the man simply let go. He dropped through the opening in the floor.

Tess screamed as she began to slip. He'd been wedged against her, supporting her weight even as he'd been trying to dislodge her grip and send her hurtling to her death. Now, supporting her own weight with her already slipping grip on the rotted wood, she was in graver danger than ever.

Maxim moved forward, stepping carefully so that he didn't cause any further damage that would make her situation more precarious. When at last he was close enough, he laid down, reaching for her and grasping her wrists. Carefully, with as much care as possible, he began to pull her up. There were jagged bits of wood protruding in every direction. She was covered in bruises and scrapes, some bleeding quite profusely. When at last he had her upper body above the floor, he hauled her the rest of the way up and pulled her back with him so that they sprawled on the part of the floor that was still reasonably sound.

"I thought you weren't going to search in here," he said.

"In the morning," she corrected. "I told you I wouldn't search this room in the morning. I never said anything about the afternoon."

Maxim shook his head. "I knew... from the moment you walked into my study, I knew."

"What did you know?" she asked, still breathless from her nearly lethal ordeal.

"That you would be trouble," he said "That your presence here would change everything... nothing would ever be the same."

"It won't be... because I don't know our ghost's name, but I think I know what she wants."

Chapter Nine

I T WAS AFTER eight o'clock by the time they found it. Tess had told him all that Calvert had confessed to—about luring the young women in with the promise of money, about his uncle's affliction, and about the unfortunate girl who'd been murdered by him after she'd refused to honor the arrangement.

Near the fireplace, they'd discovered a secret panel. After many attempts, they'd finally figured out the mechanism by which it opened. Beyond it was an opening that led into a narrow tunnel that meandered between the rooms and led to a larger opening between the chimneys. Inside that opening was a rolled up rug. Protruding from one end was a mass of dark, tangled hair, now matted with dust and dirt.

"That's her," Tess said, tears clouding her eyes. "I can't imagine… she was just put here, forgotten. No one to mourn her, no one to remember her. Thrown away like refuse."

"She will not be forgotten any longer," Maxim said. "Her remains will be buried properly. I suspect she was a local girl to start. Perhaps if we ask in the village, we may discover her name."

"I hope so. She deserves that. I know she frightened you, but I do not think that was ever her intent. I think she just desperately wanted help. She wanted to be found."

Maxim nodded, strangely moved by that thought. "I think you're right. Perhaps if I hadn't been so young when I first encountered her, I might have been able to do more—to recognize that."

"It's done now… and both Calvert and your uncle are now paying the ultimate penalty for their crimes. There is no escaping judgment in death, is there?"

Maxim nodded, then they moved away from that space, following the narrow passage back into his bedchamber. Two footmen waited there, a litter placed on the floor at their feet. "The body is in there," Maxim said. "What's left of it, at any rate. Treat it as gently as you can."

"The stable lads are building a box for her, my lord," one of the footmen replied. "It'll be ready soon. What should we do with it after?"

"Put it in the drawing room below stairs. We won't be using it for some time," he said. "I'll speak to the vicar about it in the morning and arrange for her burial."

The footmen nodded, then moved into that dark, hidden space to remove the pitiful remains of a life wasted and ruined by the selfishness of others.

"You can't sleep in here tonight," Tess whispered to him.

"I'll likely never sleep in here again," he admitted ruefully. "I may not fear her as I once did, but that doesn't mean I can ignore the fact that her body has been rotting in the walls of this chamber for two decades."

"You told me your uncle's room was damaged by a leaking roof, but that wasn't the case. Was it?"

Maxim sighed. "In his madness, he refused to ever close the windows. No matter the conditions. Even in the fiercest of storms, he'd let the rain pour in through those windows, pooling on the floor. I lied to you about the leak because—how does one explain that exactly? Until today, until Calvert confessed all to you, I didn't know the source of his madness. I worried that perhaps, since I was seeing phantoms, it might be something in our blood. Something that, one day, might claim me also."

"You're not mad… well, aside from wishing to marry a woman you hardly know," she teased. Both of them needed a moment of levity. They needed something to help them forget the horrible tragedy that they had only just uncovered.

"I know enough," he insisted. "I know that you're beautiful. And impossibly intelligent. Quite willful and hardheaded. You are also incredibly brave and I know that for the rest of our lives, we will be able to face any trial or tribulation… because surely nothing can be stranger than the circumstances which brought us together."

"You should sleep in my room," she whispered.

He grinned. "I'd already been planning to."

HOURS LATER, THEY finally managed to slip away to her chamber. The footmen had gone, taking the remains with them. One of the maids had offered up a clue as to the woman's identity. Her aunt, she said, had been missing for twenty years. Everyone had assumed she'd run off to London because she was a beautiful girl with the sort of looks that would bring her many opportunities of a disreputable nature. But no one had heard from her since. No letters. No visits. She'd simply vanished.

The timing was right. And if it was her, then her name was Lucy Gardner. Tess hoped that was true, hoped that they'd solved all of her mysteries and given her peace. The maid would be traveling to her family the following day to determine if the garments recovered from the remains could be identified as having belonged to the missing woman.

"What will you do if she is Lucy Gardner?"

Maxim looked at her from where he lounged before the window, staring out into the night. He looked like a man who had the weight of the world on his shoulders. "I will see that she has a proper burial, that some sort of compensation, bitter comfort though it may be, is provided to her family... and we will have this entire house searched top to bottom to ensure that no one else remains hidden in these walls."

"These are not your crimes... they are a terrible burden that you have inherited," she pointed out. "You were a child. You could not have stopped your uncle then. And I have no doubt that both you and your grandmother were kept far from here by your uncle and Calvert so that their misdeeds could continue undiscovered... and so that his condition could remain a secret."

He turned away from the window then, facing her fully. "I know that. I know that, ultimately, I cannot change what has happened, just as I could not prevent it. But I do not wish to speak of my uncle now. Nor do I wish to speak of that poor, unfortunate girl. In fact, Tess... I no longer wish to speak at all. There are other things that we could do right now."

Tess felt her heart begin to race. With just those words and the way his gaze moved over her, she could feel her blood heating and that same need she'd felt earlier came roaring back to life. "What sort of things did you have in mind?"

"I thought," he said, striding toward her with slow, measured steps—like a lion she'd once seen in a menagerie, "we might begin with a kiss."

"Kissing is certainly an excellent way to spend our time," she agreed.

"As a general rule," he murmured, now close enough that even a whisper could be heard, "it's the first recognizable step of seduction."

"There are unrecognizable steps of seduction?"

He reached out, taking her hand, and turned it over in his, exposing the inside of her wrist. His thumb pressed there, tracing slow circles over the pulse that beat there. "Seduction can begin with a glance, a word, a touch... you seduced me with the stubborn tilt of your chin. I found it entrancing. Irresistible, even."

She laughed. "My chin?"

"Yes," he said, a teasing glint in his eyes. "Your eyes. The tiny freckles on the crest of your right cheekbone. The perfect shell of your lovely and quite symmetrical ears. And this," he lifted her pinky. "This is the most perfect finger in all of creation. All others should be compared to it and they will all be lacking."

"One would think a more useful finger might be a better choice," she pointed out. But her voice hitched slightly as he raised her hand to his mouth and pressed a kiss to the tip of her pinky. He followed it by kissing each finger in turn, then her palm, then her wrist. At that point, she couldn't even form a coherent thought.

"Oh, it will be quite useful," he replied as he pressed her hand to his heart. "I daresay that it will take you no time at all to wind me around that perfect little finger and have me right where you want me."

Her mouth had gone dry. Nervously, she licked her lower lip. "And where is it that you think I'll want you?"

"Let me show you," he said.

Then he kissed her. Hungrily. Tenderly. With an aching need that left them both shaken and heated. His hands stroked over her body, coasting over flesh that had suddenly become unbearably sensitive. Her clothes felt too tight, abrading her skin and all she wanted was to remove them, to strip away all the many barriers that remained between them. She wanted to know what it felt like to feel his skin on hers, to touch him as he now touched her.

When her dress simply fell away, the garment somehow magically loosened by his questing fingers, she breathed a sigh of relief. Her petticoat followed and then her stays. Each garment was tossed carelessly onto the floor, but she couldn't bring herself to care.

Standing before him in only her chemise and stockings, she tugged at his coat. Obediently, he shrugged out of it, allowing it to fall to the floor. His loosened cravat was pulled free next, then his waistcoat. He broke the kiss just long enough to tug his shirt up and over his head.

There wasn't time to truly take in the perfection of his form. She had only a brief impression of hard muscles and smooth skin. But when he pulled her close, molding her form to his, she could feel the crisp hair of his chest as it brushed against her skin. And she could feel the hard ridge of his arousal pressed against her.

Maxim picked her up, scooping her into his arms with easy strength and carried her to the bed. He didn't place her on it, but settled onto it himself, arranging her legs so that she sat astride his thighs, facing him. The position opened her to him, allowed her to feel him pressed intimately against her. Then he began to peel her chemise away, sliding it off one shoulder first, then the other, shimmying it down over her arms until it pooled at her waist. The cooler air of the room made her shiver, her nipples tightening as much from the weight of his hungry gaze as the cold.

He leaned forward, pressing a kiss to the swell of one breast. The sensation of his tongue sliding over her skin as his mouth moved ever lower had her gasping. She couldn't hold back the moan that escaped her as his mouth closed over one pebbled peak. The ache that had been building inside her, that hollow feeling that would only be assuaged by having him inside her, seemed to grow beyond all reason until it overwhelmed her.

His mouth drove her wild, left her desperate, greedy for his touch. Unable to resist, she allowed her hands to roam over his chest, feeling the heat of his skin, the firmness of his muscles and the velvety texture of his skin. One of his hands slipped between them, touching her intimately, stroking that part of her that had now grown slick with need.

"Please," she whispered. "I need you, Maxim. I need you now."

"It's too soon… you aren't ready."

"I am," she said. "I am a virgin, but I am no innocent miss. I know what will happen between us. And I've been unable to think of anything else from the moment I first met you. I don't need to be seduced… I am a more than willing and eager participant." To prove her point, she let her hands travel lower, until they encountered the fall of his breeches. She paused then, for just a heartbeat, then freed the first button. Slowly, methodically, she freed each one. His entire body tensed, every muscle going rigid against her. But she kept her gaze locked on his, savoring the hunger she saw there. And when at last his breeches parted, she closed her hand around him. It was as if someone had covered steel with warm silk as she slid her hand over him, stroking him gently.

"If you do that again, this will be over before it begins," he warned her as he caught her wrist in his hand, halting her movements.

"I want to touch you… and I want you to touch me."

He let go of her wrist, slid his hand under her bottom and lifted her, moving her just slightly… and when he lowered her, she could feel him against the entrance of her body. Pressing against her—hard, insistent. It was instinct that had her sinking down slowly, his hard flesh pressing into her, filling her. That ache—that persistent, desperate ache she'd felt for so long finally began to ease.

There was no pain. Only a feeling of rightness. Of wholeness as they came together. And when he began to move inside her, lifting her easily, guiding her hips into that perfect rhythm, her back arched. Her head fell back and the sounds that escaped her were completely foreign to her. And all the while, he whispered words against her skin that, at any other time, would have made her blush. But they only added to the pleasure.

The ache that she'd thought assuaged returned—more intense, more demanding. It was accompanied by an unbearable tension, her muscles coiling tightly. She felt as if she were striving to reach something, but what it was she did not know. Every thrust brought her closer and closer to that edge. Then she understood. The tension simply snapped as pleasure washed through her. Waves of it flooded her body, leaving her limp and replete. Only seconds later, she felt him surge into her one last time, the rush and heat of his release against her sensitive flesh making her shiver. His arms closed tightly about her, holding her close as their hearts beat wildly and their ragged breathing finally settled into its natural rhythm.

"That was perfect," she said.

"It was too quick," he insisted. "I should have taken my time with you. You deserve all the pleasure I can give you."

"I don't think I could withstand more pleasure than you have already given me," she whispered. "That was beyond anything I'd ever dreamed of."

She felt him grin against her neck. Then he pressed a kiss there. "It was only the beginning, Tess. Only the beginning."

---•••◆•••---

Epilogue

Four Months Later

T HEY WERE IN London. It was the Season, but neither of them had any desire to attend the various social functions and be part of that glittering scene. They were quite content to spend their evenings quietly at home—to bask in the pleasure of one another.

Seated to Maxim's left at the small table in the breakfast room, Tess read the note from Effie, frowning slightly. When she'd finished, she filed the letter and placed it on the table. "There's no news about Lord Highcliff yet. No one has seen him since he left the Darrow School. Effie is terribly worried... what correspondence has you so enthralled?"

"It's just an update from Winters, the new butler. The household is shaping up nicely. He's eliminated some of the servants, replaced others. There have been no sightings of our phantom since Calvert— well, since Calvert. And, per the vicar, the monument for Lucy Gardner has been placed in the churchyard. She has had her proper burial and her name, at long last, has been fully returned to her. She is forgotten no more."

Tess breathed a sigh of relief. "Oh, that is wonderful news. And your grandmother's new companion?"

Maxim smiled. "She's a termagant apparently. Grandmother is no longer in charge... and no longer allowed to simply lounge in her chambers. The new companion, helpfully provided by Miss Darrow, has her attending functions and paying calls on the neighbors. There's even talk of heading to Bath for some 'real' society."

Tess couldn't hold back a giggle. "Oh, my! I'd certainly like to be a fly on the wall when those negotiations occurred."

"Negotiations! Ha. Apparently, they have full on shouting matches. Grandmother thinks it's wonderful. She says it's keeping her young."

It was the perfect opportunity, she thought. "I might have something else that will keep her young," she offered.

"And what's that?" he asked, lifting her hand to kiss it gently.

"Being a great-grandmother."

Maxim was silent. He didn't even blink. For the longest moment, he simply stared at her.

"Say something," she urged. "Are you happy?"

"I don't think happy begins to describe how I feel," he finally managed. "I am ecstatic. I am terrified. I am thankful. Joyous."

Tess let out the breath she'd been holding. "I never thought, when marrying you after only a few days' acquaintance, that we could be this happy. And now you'll have a son."

"Or a daughter... with auburn hair and the perfect amount of freckles," he suggested. "She'll be beautiful and brave like her mother and I will love her to distraction... as I love her mother."

Tess' heartbeat skipped in her chest. He'd never said those words to her before. Just as she'd never been quite brave enough to say them to him, though she'd felt them every day. They'd crept through her mind time and time again and hovered on the tip of her tongue. Fear had held her in check. "I love you, Maxim. I love you so much. I can't imagine my life without you."

"You'll never have to," he said. He reached out and tapped her little finger where it rested against the tabletop. "I'm always right there. Perfectly wrapped around your finger."

Tess began to laugh, feeling giddy with joy. Things had been so dark in the beginning. But now it was all light and joy. "I wouldn't have it any other way."

The End

About the Author

Chasity Bowlin lives in central Kentucky with her husband and their menagerie of animals. She loves writing, loves traveling and enjoys incorporating tidbits of her actual vacations into her books. She is an avid Anglophile, loving all things British, but specifically all things Regency.

Growing up in Tennessee, spending as much time as possible with her doting grandparents, soap operas were a part of her daily existence, followed by back to back episodes of Scooby Doo. Her path to becoming a romance novelist was set when, rather than simply have her Barbie dolls cruise around in a pink convertible, they time traveled, hosted lavish dinner parties and one even had an evil twin locked in the attic.

Website: www.chasitybowlin.com

Printed in Great Britain
by Amazon

41334952R00040